ISBN: 978-1-7371099-6-9

Library of Congress Control Number: 2023905520

Manufactured in the United States

Any resemblance to actual events or persons, living or dead, is entirely coincidental. This is in no form meant for harm nor do we promote harm. Personal perspective use only. Please do not copy/ mimic any words or illustration from this book.

Illustrations by Cameron Wilson for Soulsimplicity Design and Publishing.

"This book is dedicated to my parents, who have passed away. Thank you for never stifling the creative spirit within me and always nurturing my imagination".

-Pocahontas Carter

MIND GAMES
TV OF THINGS
BY POCAHONTAS CARTER
ILLUSTRATED BY CAMERON WILSON

One Saturday, Zac and his family went to the county fair.
They met a little old lady with wispy white hair.
She looked like she had left her teeth in the dentist's chair.
Her memory did not seem to be all there.
Maybe that day, it was hiding somewhere.

She said, "My name is Louise. I sell remote control trucks, lawnmowers, and TVs."

Zac's dad saw a television that looked like one he used as a child. The TV had a bent antenna and two rickety old knobs for the dial.

Mrs. Louise was a kind-hearted soul.
She offered to include a gaming console.
The television was old and out-of-date,
but somehow Mrs. Louise got it to operate.
Fiddling with the channels,
she explained that the TV could turn into an airplane.
She believed what she said,
but that look did not convince MeMaw or Dad.

Once they got home,
Zac's dad connected the TV to the game console.
Then positioned the antennas in the attic.
The television turned on by itself
-buzzing loud with static.
The TV could only get channels
two, three, seven, and sixteen.

A lady and a boy walked,
holding hands and eating ice cream.
The ground rumbles, tremors, and shakes,
and the ground starts to break.
A basketball pole began to grow out of a hole.
They both became alarmed.
Then a basketball fell from the sky into the boy's arms!
Basketball was his favorite thing! He was thrilled.
Especially after a voice shouted,
"Show me your basketball skills!"

He handed his ice cream cone to his mother.
He dribbled the ball under one leg
and then under the other.
The boy sprinted down the court to do a slam dunk
while the camera zoomed in for a close-up.
He had big brown eyes, a mole on his nose,
and a wide silly grin. His cheeks had a rosy glow,
and he looked familiar, like someone I know.

Swoosh, swoosh, swoosh-three points for the win!
He turned his back to the hoop
and threw the ball over his shoulder,
and the ball still went in!
If channel seven was this much fun for free,
Zac had to see what mystery was on channel three.
Channel three was clear and sharp.

Zac was face-to-face with Iris,
the flower shop owner in the book,
The Flowers in the Shop.
She handed him a magical flower with a superpower
that could turn frogs into humans for an hour!

Zac switched the TV back to channel two.
He invited frogs to come to play who were eating Stinkaroo Stew.
Zac only asked two, but to his amazement,
six frogs leaped through.
Zac could not believe what he was seeing.
Six little frogs had turned into human beings!

They put that hour into good use.
They played Zac's favorite game,
Duck, Duck, Goose.
They played hide and seek, tug of war,
and a game they made up, Theodore,
the crazy two-headed dinosaur!

Zac was feeling a little sad when the frogs had to go.
So, he switched the console
to TV mode to watch his favorite TV show.
As soon as he turned to channel sixteen,
The television sucked Zac into the TV screen!

Zac inside the TV did not make any sense,
but here lies the evidence.
Zac was watching TV and eating pistachios;
in a blink of an eye, the portal opened and closed.
Zac had no clue how to stop the ride
without an instruction guide.

Zac dips, glides, slips, and slides.
It bobbles, it wobbles, and it is not stable.
The TV should have had a warning label.
It had a steering wheel and controls inside;
boy, was he having fun on that airplane ride.
Zac was zipping and zooming,
having a fun fest in the Tiny Tots Air Express!

"Mrs. Louise is the best," he exclaimed with delight!
Zac's mom kissed his forehead and tucked him in bed for the night.
Suddenly, Zac sat straight up in the bed and said,
"It just hit me, that kid holding Memaw's hand was my dad!"

Dad was the child with the big eyes,
the mole on his nose, and the silly grin.
He must have had a magical portal to play in!
That night Zac's love for his dad made
his heart grow ten times its size.
He wanted to be just like his dad, strong, brave, and wise.

Zac's dad donated the TV to Zac's school.
Now, any child can be a pilot during recess.
If you do not believe it, put it to the test.
Close your eyes, hold on tight
and let your imagination do the rest.

The End.

SCHOOL

CHILDREN'S CHAT

1. Where did Zac and his family go when he met the little old lady, Louise?

2. Mrs. Louise left her _______________ in the dentist's chair.

3. What jumped out of the TV to play with Zac?

4. Who was the child with the big eyes, the mole on his nose, and the silly grin?

5. What was your favorite part of the story?

6. You are sitting at home watching your favorite TV show, and suddenly, the TV sucks you inside. What would you do for fun while you are stuck inside?

Let's spark your kiddo's imagination! Please share your adventures with us on our website and become part of our pretend-play family!

HokeyPoquii.com

ABOUT THE AUTHOR

Pocahontas Carter is a glam-ma and a mother of four. She is a woman of color with plenty of life lessons to use as a pathway towards the nurturing, growing, and expansion of little traveling minds. Traveling minds can take you places, and Pocahontas Carter invites you, the reader, to travel with her into a world where her creative thoughts turn into words on paper. She is a DC native, attended John Burroughs Elementary and Taft Junior High. A graduate of McKinley Tech Senior High School ("Go –Trainers!"), she writes in a rhyming fashion with colorful illustrations and promotes empowerment through children's literature.